Acting Edition

That Which Isn't

by Matthew Freeman

Copyright © 2017 by Matthew Freeman
All Rights Reserved

THAT WHICH ISN'T is fully protected under the copyright laws of the United States of America, the British Commonwealth, including Canada, and all member countries of the Berne Convention for the Protection of Literary and Artistic Works, the Universal Copyright Convention, and/or the World Trade Organization conforming to the Agreement on Trade Related Aspects of Intellectual Property Rights. All rights, including professional and amateur stage productions, recitation, lecturing, public reading, motion picture, radio broadcasting, television, online/digital production, and the rights of translation into foreign languages are strictly reserved.

ISBN 978-0-573-70656-1

www.concordtheatricals.com
www.concordtheatricals.co.uk

FOR PRODUCTION INQUIRIES

UNITED STATES AND CANADA
info@concordtheatricals.com
1-866-979-0447

UNITED KINGDOM AND EUROPE
licensing@concordtheatricals.co.uk
020-7054-7298

Each title is subject to availability from Concord Theatricals Corp., depending upon country of performance. Please be aware that *THAT WHICH ISN'T* may not be licensed by Concord Theatricals Corp. in your territory. Professional and amateur producers should contact the nearest Concord Theatricals Corp. office or licensing partner to verify availability.

CAUTION: Professional and amateur producers are hereby warned that *THAT WHICH ISN'T* is subject to a licensing fee. The purchase, renting, lending or use of this book does not constitute a license to perform this title(s), which license must be obtained from Concord Theatricals Corp. prior to any performance. Performance of this title(s) without a license is a violation of federal law and may subject the producer and/or presenter of such performances to civil penalties. Both amateurs and professionals considering a production are strongly advised to apply to the appropriate agent before starting rehearsals, advertising, or booking a theatre. A licensing fee must be paid whether the title(s) is presented for charity or gain and whether or not admission is charged. Professional/Stock licensing fees are quoted upon application to Concord Theatricals Corp.

This work is published by Samuel French, an imprint of Concord Theatricals Corp.

No one shall make any changes in this title(s) for the purpose of production. No part of this book may be reproduced, stored in a retrieval system, scanned, uploaded, or transmitted in any form, by any means, now known or yet to be invented, including mechanical, electronic, digital, photocopying, recording, videotaping, or otherwise, without the prior written permission of the publisher. No one shall share this title(s), or any part of this title(s), through any social media or file hosting websites.

For all inquiries regarding motion picture, television, online/digital and other media rights, please contact Concord Theatricals Corp.

MUSIC AND THIRD-PARTY MATERIALS USE NOTE

Licensees are solely responsible for obtaining formal written permission from copyright owners to use copyrighted music and/or other copyrighted third-party materials (e.g. artworks, logos) in the performance of this play and are strongly cautioned to do so. If no such permission is obtained by the licensee, then the licensee must use only original music and materials that the licensee owns and controls. Licensees are solely responsible and liable for clearances of all third-party copyrighted materials, including without limitation music, and shall indemnify the copyright owners of the play(s) and their licensing agent, Concord Theatricals Corp., against any costs, expenses, losses and liabilities arising from the use of such copyrighted third-party materials by licensees. For music, please contact the appropriate music licensing authority in your territory for the rights to any incidental music.

IMPORTANT BILLING AND CREDIT REQUIREMENTS

If you have obtained performance rights to this title, please refer to your licensing agreement for important billing and credit requirements.

THAT WHICH ISN'T was originally produced at the Brick Theater in Brooklyn, New York from August 11 to August 20, 2016. It was produced by Theater Accident (Matthew Freeman and Kyle Ancowitz) and directed by Kyle Ancowitz, with set design by Kerry Lee Chipman, lighting design by Nicholas Houfek, and costumes by Jonna McElrath. The stage manager was Jodi Witherell and the assistant director was Jordan Barsky. The cast was as follows:

HELEN...Moira Stone
JAMES / WAITER................................. David DelGrosso
MARCUS ....Mick O'Brien

CHARACTERS

HELEN – a woman in her early and then later thirties
JAMES – a man in his early thirties
MARCUS – a man in his early forties
WAITER – thirties

SETTING

An open field outside an East Coast city.
A restaurant in Los Angeles.

TIME

One day, and five years later.

For John Walsh.

ACT ONE

Scene One

(HELEN and JAMES sit under a tree.)
(The tree is alone in an open field.)
(Dusk.)

JAMES. This tree. What kind of tree would you say it is?

HELEN. Hard to say.

JAMES. It's not that hard to say. I just didn't know if you knew. You tend to know about stuff like this.

HELEN. I don't know. Fir. Pine. Something like that.

JAMES. Okay.

(Pause.)

I didn't mean to offend you.

HELEN. Why would it offend me?

JAMES. Not offend. Not offend.

HELEN. Why are we even talking about this?

JAMES. I don't know.

(Pause.)

It's dark.

HELEN. I like it.

JAMES. I do too.

HELEN. So that's one thing.

JAMES. It is.

HELEN. And we both like the tree.

JAMES. I didn't say I liked it. I just asked what kind it is.

HELEN. But you do like it.

JAMES. I guess I like it. I don't have opinions about things I can't change.

HELEN. Do you have a favorite color?

JAMES. I do.

HELEN. And you have a favorite movie?

JAMES. Yes.

HELEN. So what you just said doesn't make any sense.

JAMES. I guess not.

HELEN. So do you want to revise what you said? Maybe?

JAMES. Not really.

HELEN. Why not?

JAMES. No reason.

HELEN. And the tree?

JAMES. I like it.

(Pause.)

HELEN. Good. Me too.

(Pause.)

A sycamore.

JAMES. You don't know.

(Pause.)

I don't think I actually care what kind of tree it is. You just tend to know about these kinds of things.

HELEN. You don't have to make conversation.

JAMES. What else am I going to do?

HELEN. You just don't have to. That's all.

JAMES. What's the alternative?

HELEN. Silence.

JAMES. You'd prefer that?

HELEN. Maybe I would.

JAMES. Would you?

HELEN. No.

(Pause.)

Well, yes.
> *(Pause.)*

I guess it depends on what we're talking about.

JAMES. Just allow me to...ease into things. For once.
HELEN. Do what you will.
JAMES. Thank you.
> *(Pause.)*

I think it's a maple.
HELEN. Nobody asked you.
> *(Pause.)*

And I'm sure you're wrong.
> *(Blackout.)*

Scene Two

*(**HELEN** is standing, looking up. **JAMES** sits.)*

HELEN. When's the last time you climbed a tree?

JAMES. I don't know.

HELEN. I haven't done it in a long time. I guess that's what the city does. Makes trees something to look at, not play with.

JAMES. I like it in the city.

HELEN. I know.

JAMES. You don't like it?

HELEN. I just miss climbing trees. I was tiny, and I could get way high up, and the tree wouldn't even bend. I was that light.

JAMES. I just don't like the idea of falling and dying.

HELEN. Right.

JAMES. The tree can't take my weight.

HELEN. It might. If you'd give it a go.

JAMES. Why risk it?

HELEN. For fun?

JAMES. Is that fun? To climb a tree?

HELEN. It used to be.

(Pause.)

JAMES. It used to be.

(Pause.)

You wanted us to move. I know that.

HELEN. It doesn't matter.

JAMES. I like the apartment.

HELEN. Well, that's good. Because no one is making you leave it.

(Pause.)

I remember risk as something you're perfectly comfortable with. Or at least, I thought so. Or at least, it seemed so.

JAMES. Seemed so? Seems so.

HELEN. Seemed. I think is the way I'd put it.

JAMES. Back when? Before now? When I was young.

HELEN. I don't want to play this game. I don't want to talk about verb tenses with you. No, is the answer, to whatever you're getting at. I just wanted to talk about climbing trees.

> *(Pause.)*

Do you want to talk about that?

> *(Pause.)*

Where did you go?

JAMES. I'm here.

HELEN. I know. But where did you go?

> *(Blackout.)*

Scene Three

*(**JAMES** and **HELEN** lying on the ground. Darker.)*

HELEN. The whole place was wall-to-wall cups. Little tea cups and coffee mugs and those tall sort of not-really wine glasses, if you know what I mean. I think she thought of it as a collection, but it wasn't a collection. It wasn't really a collection of anything. It was organized in no way I could imagine. Well, I guess it could be that anything she'd recently bought was closest to the entrance. There were a few I recognized from when fast food restaurants used to give away actual glasses, made of glass, with happy meals. For promotions. We had all these cups from movies. Family movies.

(Pause.)

I asked her what she intended to do with all these mugs and cups and she said she'd sell them, she thought, or give them away. She liked them. She said she has a friend with lots of shoes, like this, but she never really liked shoes.

(Pause.)

I told her that she was going to have to make decisions about these things, now. Even write it all down, if she wanted. She knew that we were going to try to sell that house, make her go somewhere they could take care of her, but she didn't like to talk about it. So that was hard.

(Pause.)

She couldn't argue against it, but she was scared of it, and didn't want to live that way. I get it. I wish we didn't have to make her live that way. But she can't stay with me. My brother? He doesn't even know what's going on.

(Pause.)

She said she wanted me to have them, so I could sell them. But I can't sell them, they're junk. I could put them out for a yard sale, but she might see. I don't know. I wish she hadn't told me to take them. I don't want them.

>   *(Pause.)*

Isn't that sad?

JAMES. It is.

HELEN. Are you listening?

JAMES. I am.

HELEN. Does it make you sad?

JAMES. It doesn't make me sad. But it is sad.

>   *(Blackout.)*

Scene Four

    (**JAMES** *and* **HELEN**, *standing up. Night.*)

HELEN. I like people.

JAMES. You don't.

HELEN. Yes I do.

JAMES. You have to go to therapy for three days a week just to deal with them.

HELEN. That's not about them. It's about me.

JAMES. Is it possible that it's about them? That you can't understand people? That when they talk or move around, it's like you're watching bears make noise at the zoo?

    (Pause.)

Remember that time when we were at Sam's and Sam's girlfriend kept talking about working out? After the party, you said, "Who does that? Who talks about going to the gym? Why would someone do that?" And I thought to myself, "Everyone. Most people." If someone says, "Oh I went to the shore today!" you wonder why you're being told.

HELEN. What am I supposed to do with that information? They went to the shore. I didn't. So why tell me?

JAMES. Because people talk to each other. About mundane things. For fun. Or because if you keep everything you do or did to yourself, then no one knows anything about you.

HELEN. Is that what happens when you keep things to yourself? People don't feel like they know who you are?

    (Pause.)

JAMES. I said everything. I said when you keep everything to yourself.

HELEN. So, share the mundane things. Feign interest. The important things? What are we supposed to do with those?

(Pause.)

JAMES. Some things, you don't have to explain over and over. Some things just are the way they are. To ask certain questions is to be…incredulous. About…nothing. Air.

(Pause.)

You know how I make up stories for Edie?

HELEN. Yes.

JAMES. Well, think of it as not having to make up fake stories. Because you have real ones. That's all it is.

HELEN. I wish you wouldn't talk to me like this.

JAMES. I know.

HELEN. I'm just a normal person.

JAMES. No you're not.

HELEN. I wish you wouldn't make me feel abnormal.

JAMES. I wish you had a sense of humor about being abnormal.

HELEN. You think I go to therapy because I find myself hilarious?

JAMES. You are pretty funny.

HELEN. I'm not funny. This isn't funny. You aren't being funny.

JAMES. Yes I am. I'm being very funny.

(Pause.)

You want me to treat you with kid gloves?

HELEN. You should.

JAMES. I won't.

HELEN. You shouldn't. You don't. You won't. You should.

JAMES. You don't actually want me to.

(Pause.)

HELEN. No I don't.

(Pause.)

But you should.

(Blackout.)

Scene Five

(HELEN *lays with her head on* JAMES' *lap.*)

JAMES. The princess was taller than all the other people in the kingdom. Not a giant, really. Just tall. Tall and lanky and awkward. Impressively tall. Wonderfully tall.

(Pause.)

But…because of this…she didn't fit into the kingdom. Not because she acted differently or thought differently. No, she was as normal as anyone else. She just didn't fit. In her clothes. In doorways. In her royal carriage. She wondered if there was any way for her to sit at a table without feeling her knees knock up against the wood, or if she'd ever kiss a boy without him standing on a stool.

(Pause.)

It was spring, and so it was time for the ladies and men to do their ritual of springtime.

HELEN. Is this going to be a sex story?

JAMES. No.

HELEN. You're sure?

JAMES. No. I mean yes.

HELEN. Fine.

(Pause.)

You may proceed.

JAMES. So they were preparing and getting all decked out in fancy things. Purple gowns that shimmered. The men all wore these special shoes that had feathers that stuck up all the way to their knees. Special and wow, you have no idea how lovely these shoes were. You know? The best shoes ever. Dainty, feathered, shoes for men. Made by hand in accordance with each family…crest.

(Pause.)

The princess showed up to be fitted, and unfortunately, the gown was too short.

This was her fifteenth spring, a sort of quinceañera, and she had been so excited. She wanted to make an impression, something that showed she was entering womanhood, and didn't want it to turn into a farce just because the tailors had forgotten to bring enough cloth. Because, as I said, she was very tall.

   (Pause.)

So, she went to a man in the village that shaved men's beards. And she talked to him in private and gave him lots of gold, because she's a princess, so she had plenty of gold.

   (Pause.)

That night, oh the spring ritual was delightful. The cool air whipped around them, and they all came together around the single tree that towered over the village. They took turns circling the tree, and the men shook their shoe feathers and the women spun in their gowns, and each drank from a unique cup that was theirs and theirs alone.

   (Pause.)

Finally, the tall princess emerged. They gasped, they did, and stood in amazement. Seven feet tall, wearing men's garments, shoes feathered. She smiled, proud, her white teeth flashing. And bald. Bald as the moon in spring.

   (Pause.)

That's all I can think of.

HELEN. I liked that one.
JAMES. Can I kiss you?
HELEN. Yes.
JAMES. Not because…
HELEN. I know.

   *(**HELEN** kisses him.)*

Bald as the moon in spring.

   (Blackout.)

Scene Six

(**JAMES** *and* **HELEN** *are beneath the tree, wrapped in each other's arms. They kiss and touch each other. They are barely visible.* **HELEN** *laughs a little.*)

Scene Seven

(**JAMES** *is alone onstage. He looks up at the tree. The black sky. Smiles. Then stops smiling.*)

(**HELEN** *enters.*)

HELEN. You have to go a long way to pee somewhere private.

JAMES. You didn't have to run off.

HELEN. I don't like being watched.

JAMES. Also? I can't see you more than ten feet that way. It's too dark.

HELEN. You could hear. I don't like being heard.

JAMES. Well, problem solved. Just go far away.

(Pause.)

(**JAMES** *seems to want to say something, and then doesn't.* **HELEN** *can tell, and saves him.*)

HELEN. That was nice.

JAMES. I think it was sad.

HELEN. It didn't make me sad.

(Pause.)

But it is sad.

(Blackout.)

Scene Eight

(HELEN sits downstage, apart from JAMES, facing the audience.)

HELEN. My brother called this morning before we drove up.

JAMES. He okay?

HELEN. No. Not really.

(Pause.)

Did I tell you he's going to move to Canada?

JAMES. Because of what?

HELEN. Something he heard on the radio. He's angry with the United States. It's a thing to be angry with.

JAMES. Well, that's up to him I guess.

HELEN. I don't think he'll actually do it. He can barely remember to change the oil in his car.

JAMES. He's already halfway across the country. Who knows?

(Pause.)

He might be closer. When it's all said and done.

HELEN. When it's all said and done. Because, you know, that's an eventuality. All things being said. All things being done.

(Pause.)

I don't know. I guess that could be better.

JAMES. Far is far is far.

HELEN. I'm just glad he doesn't have to move in with me. I couldn't handle that.

JAMES. What does your mom say?

HELEN. She doesn't say.

JAMES. Helpful as always.

HELEN. Don't talk about her.

JAMES. I know, I know.

HELEN. She's doing the best she can.

JAMES. The very best? The best she can?

(Pause.)

HELEN. See, you think you're taking my side when you talk that way. But they're my family.

JAMES. They are.

HELEN. If you wanted to be on my side, you wouldn't take sides against them.

JAMES. How many sides are there?

HELEN. There are no sides. That's what I'm trying to say.

JAMES. There are too many sides. That's the problem.

HELEN. There are no sides. She's my mother. She's not a side. Not an adversary.

JAMES. She should help you.

HELEN. But she won't. She won't, so why wait for that? Why insist on that? Why remind me of how she isn't, when she is other things. Like loving. Like trying hard. Like brave. She's had cancer twice. She quit drinking. She's lonely.

JAMES. Your brother was arrested in her house, okay? And so she washes her hands of it. And it's your problem?

HELEN. Yes.

JAMES. Is that fair?

HELEN. What are you? Twelve?

JAMES. It's not fair. You're not outraged. You're not protecting yourself.

HELEN. You think that angry is the same thing as armor. It's actually harder for me not to be angry. I'm working harder than anyone else, you know. To keep myself from being angry with all of them. Which is what you're not helping.

(Pause.)

Anyway, I don't want him to move away. I don't care. I'd rather he not leave.

(Pause.)

It's really dark. I like the sounds out here. It's actually loud, a little. The insects. They make a lot of noise.

JAMES. They do.

HELEN. I always think, when I'm at home, that somewhere else it's silent and I miss the silence. Then, I guess, I realize, there's no such thing as silence.

JAMES. I'm sure there is…artificial silence. Silence in comparison to other things. A sort of silence.

HELEN. There really is no such thing.

    (Pause.)

You used to say I gave you The Silence. As a punishment. When I thought you were being selfish.

JAMES. I did.

HELEN. But I wasn't silent.

JAMES. No.

HELEN. I wasn't ever silent.

JAMES. No.

HELEN. You could always hear me.

JAMES. I will always hear you. Even years from now, when I can barely hear, I'll be able to hear you.

HELEN. What does that mean?

JAMES. It means something to me.

HELEN. I wish you wouldn't try so hard.

JAMES. I wish you would try harder.

    (Pause.)

You cut your leg.

HELEN. Oh?

    (She looks.)

Oh.

JAMES. I noticed it a while ago. But I didn't say anything.

    (Pause.)

Does it hurt?

HELEN. Not until you pointed it out.

JAMES. Isn't that funny?

HELEN. Well, it would be. If it didn't hurt.

    (Blackout.)

Scene Nine

(**HELEN** *alone onstage. She doesn't move. She looks straight forward, over the audience, into the dark.*)

(*Blackout.*)

Scene Ten

(**JAMES** *is standing against the tree.* **HELEN** *is leaning against his legs.*)

JAMES. She says that we need to circle back and reconvene when the time is right to discuss annual reviews. She asks me if I've completed my 360 review, and I say that when George had his review, they literally used his anonymous, supposedly anonymous, comments as a part of his assessment and that means that no, I won't be participating because I don't trust the process. Who would? She did that frown thing, she's English, so she frowns in an English accent, you know? Disappointed in the kids, that sort of thing. She said that George wasn't supposed to be discussing his assessment anyway, and she's been assured that the comments are anonymous. Besides, the 360 is mandatory. That's what she said. You know what I said? Mandatory as in what? I'll be fired? If I won't be fired, it's not mandatory.

(*Pause.*)

She told me that mandatory didn't mean fired, it meant it's not optional, and I said that I know the literal definition of the word. I said the meaning, though, of the word in this context is to create a sense of coercion even though there's no stick. No carrot, no stick, no incentives, the illusion of something compulsory. Their only tactic is the power of suggestion. The only consequence is I'll be asked to do it again, and I'll refuse again. I told her that I'd worked there for eight years, and that I felt no need to be told what's what. I told her that I would be happy to be reviewed, sure, and to hear their constructive criticism, yes, but no, I wouldn't be participating.

(*Pause.*)

I mean, they refuse to give us raises, and they sell the company and take the company public, and then it's off the market and the private equity company slices off our heads, and we all survive that and then it's...don't forget to fill out the form!

>   *(Pause.)*

Fuck her, is my point.

HELEN. So are you fired?

JAMES. Not yet.

HELEN. They'll fire you.

JAMES. I wish they would already.

HELEN. Me too. You've told me this story every year for five years.

>   *(Pause.)*

I think, after it's all set up, and we signed everything, I'm going to move away.

>   *(Pause.)*

I can't afford to right now. But I need to get away.

>   *(Pause.)*

JAMES. I could never leave.

>   *(Pause.)*

I love the city. I do. I like it a lot.

>   *(Pause.)*

There are lots of museums. You know?

>   *(Pause.)*

I mean, more reasons than that. But...yeah.

HELEN. That's true. There are lots of museums.

>   *(Pause.)*

JAMES. Where would you go?

HELEN. That's the thing. Vermont, maybe? But then it's the winters and I'd commit suicide. Or I could go to just another city, like, I could move to Philly or Boston, but then why move? If it's just another version of what I'm already doing. I guess I could try San Francisco.

JAMES. That far?

HELEN. I don't know. I don't know. I just need out.

>   *(Pause.)*

To be away.

>   *(Pause.)*

Don't you?

JAMES. No.

>   *(Pause.)*

San Francisco.

>   *(Pause.)*

I was in Boise, Idaho this one time and I loved it. Can you believe that? Most of the state is a wasteland but Boise is kind of lovely.

HELEN. Are you suggesting I move to Idaho?

JAMES. It's a nice place. That's all. I sometimes forget I've ever been there, and that I liked it so much. But I just remembered, so I told you.

HELEN. Gee thanks.

JAMES. Many happy returns on the day.

HELEN. You know what I've heard about Idaho?

JAMES. What?

HELEN. Nothing.

>   *(Pause.)*

You know what I've heard about San Francisco?

JAMES. Lots of museums?

HELEN. You'd love it. Is my point.

>   *(Pause.)*

Maybe you should move.

>   *(Pause.)*

Is my point.

>   *(Blackout.)*

Scene Eleven

(They sit, close together.)

JAMES. So tell me about Richard.

HELEN. Do you really want to know about that?

JAMES. Yes.

HELEN. Don't make me do that. Can we just not fight?

JAMES. Why is it a fight?

HELEN. You're trying to pick a fight.

JAMES. I'm not.

HELEN. You are.

(Pause.)

JAMES. What's he do?

(Pause.)

How many legs does he have?

(Pause.)

Why doesn't he like little kids?

(Pause.)

What's wrong with his left eye? Why does his hair fall out in the sun? What's with all the radiation sickness? Why does Richard seem to cough a lot? Is he sick? How many kinds of flowers has Richard destroyed with his unethical business? Richard works out too much and it makes me worry that he's vain.

I remember reading this story in the *New York Post* about a rapist of children. The picture looked like Richard's face. Has he said anything about it?

HELEN. *(Laughing.)* Stop it.

JAMES. I saw a signpost that said Beware Richard. Richard's name, shortened, is Dick. Does that mean his dick is short? A long Dick is spelled Richard, therefore. Richard killed my dog, but I didn't like my dog, so tell Richard "thank you" for me. Once, I saw Richard poison something. Does it matter what he poisoned? He's a poisoner. Shouldn't that be written down about

Richard? Kept in Richard's file? Richard has bad taste in ties. Richard has strong arms, for hugging his parents with, because he fucks his parents and he lets them fuck him. Richard created the whole concept of being fucked by your parents. He called it "incest." Look it up. Richard sells slave labor for guns. Richard sells guns to children in Africa. Richard hates Africans. Richard's a racist.

(Pause.)

Do I have it about right?

HELEN. You're the one that introduced us.

JAMES. I did?

HELEN. Andrea's party in New Hampshire.

(Pause.)

The man with the...

JAMES. With the white hair? That guy?

(Pause.)

Oh.

(Pause.)

He's old.

HELEN. I like him.

JAMES. He's old.

HELEN. I'm not going to fight with you about this.

(Pause.)

But yes. He's old.

(Blackout.)

Scene Twelve

(HELEN is pacing. JAMES is lying on his back.)

HELEN. What time is it?
JAMES. It's late.
HELEN. We need to get to the car.
JAMES. We will.
HELEN. I wanted us to work.
JAMES. I know.
HELEN. I didn't want us not to work.
JAMES. No one ever wanted it not to work. But I didn't…

(Pause.)

I won't apologize again.
HELEN. Good. I don't really like how I feel when you apologize.
JAMES. Then I won't apologize.

(Pause.)

Thanks for kissing me. Thanks for coming with me out here.
HELEN. Thanks for being with me out here.

(Pause.)

JAMES. You said, remember, when we were deciding…

(Pause.)

That you never understood why I was so angry with you. I said over and over I'm not angry with you. I wasn't angry with you. I'm not angry with you.

(Pause.)

How can I say that in a way that…how can I make you believe that?
HELEN. You can't.
JAMES. You're angry with me.
HELEN. Yes. Which is normal. To be furious.
JAMES. Furious. I know. But I was never angry with you.
HELEN. All that money.

JAMES. I know.

HELEN. What kind of person does something like that?

JAMES. Whatever kind of person I am.

HELEN. We're not going to re-argue the case. No, no. I'm not having this conversation. We're not having this conversation right now. Certain things happened, other things didn't. You want things to have happened in another way. They didn't. There's one way it happened, so there's no use going over it again, thinking about maybe it could have been otherwise, because it isn't. It's one way, only this one way, and that's…

(Pause.)

We need to get to the car. I don't know whose field this is, or when they'll wake up, or what.

JAMES. Everything belongs to someone. Is there such a thing as an open field to just go lie down in?

HELEN. Somewhere, yes, but not here.

(Pause.)

JAMES. I think someday, we'll be together again.

(Pause.)

I know I'm not supposed to say that, but I wanted to say that.

(Pause.)

Do you have anything to say about that?

HELEN. No, I don't.

JAMES. Well.

(Pause.)

I understand. I understand why you don't.

HELEN. I can't talk about someday. I can talk about yesterday and I can talk about now.

(Pause.)

JAMES. You're tired.

HELEN. I'm sad.

JAMES. Are you?

HELEN. What do you think?

JAMES. I can't tell.

HELEN. That about sums it up. You can't tell. You think we'll be together again someday. Can you believe yourself when you say things like that?

JAMES. I don't know what to say.

HELEN. You don't know what to say? But that doesn't stop you. From saying whatever comes to mind.

JAMES. I say what I mean. I say what I think. I don't know.

HELEN. Those things are not the same.

JAMES. They're similar.

HELEN. No they're not. What you think and what you mean. Do not come out the same way. So they're not the same thing.

JAMES. You're angry.

>   *(Pause.)*

You're sad.

>   *(Pause.)*

You want me to stop talking.

>   *(Pause.)*

Do you want me to stop talking?

HELEN. You treat me like an inkblot.

JAMES. What?

HELEN. I'm not an inkblot, Jim. I'm not a Rorschach test. I'm not multiple choice. I'm Helen.

>   *(Pause.)*

Remember me?

JAMES. I was asking. Only asking.

HELEN. Well I'm sorry, but I can't help you. I'm sorry. But you're on your own.

>   *(Pause.)*

We need to get to the car.

>   *(Blackout.)*

Scene Thirteen

*(**JAMES** onstage, alone. **HELEN** is just offstage.)*

(It's close to early.)

JAMES. Remember when we went to Florida to see your parents, and the whole area, what is it? Saratoga?

HELEN. *(Offstage.)* Sarasota.

JAMES. Was a testament to Ringling Brothers? A circus. A whole town for the circus. I just…guess there are times I forget how many people there are in the world, and how many places there are. That there's some town somewhere, and the people of that town are completely focused on their industry, which is horseshoes. Or the history of the helmet. Or fermentation.

*(**HELEN** enters. She gathers up her shoes. She finds them behind the tree.)*

HELEN. There you are.

(She holds up the shoes.)

Found them. The devils.

JAMES. Good. Good.

HELEN. I liked that trip too. Sarasota. You always call it Saratoga. That's New York.

JAMES. Close enough.

HELEN. No. Not really.

(A kiss on the cheek.)

Time for the car. The car for you.

JAMES. Sun. See it?

(He points.)

HELEN. It's nice.

JAMES. It is nice.

HELEN. I like the air.

JAMES. I do too.

HELEN. But we have to go.

JAMES. We do.

When will I see you again?

HELEN. We have the whole drive.

JAMES. After that?

HELEN. It'll be a while.

(Pause.)

Which is good. For you. For you, not just me.

(Pause.)

JAMES. All right then.

(Pause.)

I like the air out here.

HELEN. You'd never want to come and live out here would you?

JAMES. With you?

HELEN. Ever. With anyone. By yourself.

(Pause.)

JAMES. No.

(Pause.)

But it's nice right now.

(Blackout.)

Scene Fourteen

(Dawn.)
(HELEN is in the tree.)
(JAMES is below, keeping his distance.)

JAMES. You're going to get hurt.
HELEN. Come up.
JAMES. There's no room.
HELEN. Come up!
JAMES. There's no room for both of us.
HELEN. There's room. I'll make room.
JAMES. Come on. No. I'm not coming up.
HELEN. Come up.

(Pause.)

I'm going higher.
JAMES. You'll fall.
HELEN. Encourage me, okay?

(Pause.)

Encourage me.
JAMES. Go higher! You can do it!
HELEN. That's the spirit.
JAMES. But don't fall on me. You'll kill me.
HELEN. That's the spirit. I'll kill you.

(She climbs higher.)

I think that's about as far as I'm going.

(She perches, looks up and out.)

The thing is, I actually can't see all that much more up here than I could down there. It's a field. There's the road. There's that hardware warehouse.
JAMES. Well what did you expect?
HELEN. Maybe I could see...another woman, in a tree, looking back at me, with a guy, looking up at her. Us,

far off in the distance. And we – me and I – would see each other and wave at each other. Or just stare. Because we don't know if we should wave. Because…if we wave at the same time…what does that mean?

(Pause.)

But no.

JAMES. You should come down.

HELEN. Or you'll what?

JAMES. Or I'll nothing.

HELEN. That's right. You'll nothing.

(Pause.)

Why don't you even try to come up here?

JAMES. It literally cannot be done. There is nowhere that I'll fit. The tree won't hold me. Take your pick.

(Pause.)

HELEN. Coward.

(Pause.)

You'd love it up here.

(Blackout.)

End of Act One

ACT TWO

Scene One

(Five years later.)

*(**MARCUS**, a man in his early forties, sits alone at a quiet table in a quiet restaurant. He looks at the menu, touches his cutlery, drinks some water, and then looks at his phone.)*

(He texts someone.)

(He looks at his menu.)

(He stares at the empty seat in front of him.)

*(Enter **HELEN**.)*

(She looks extremely composed and professional. It may take a moment to register she's the same character from Act One.)

(She begins speaking the moment she enters, takes off her coat, and puts down her purse.)

HELEN. I'm so sorry. I'm really sorry.

*(**MARCUS** rises to meet her.)*

MARCUS. It's all right. I haven't been here long. Can I…

*(It's not clear if **MARCUS** means "take your coat." **HELEN** gives him a firm handshake instead.)*

HELEN. No, I've got it. Thank you.

MARCUS. Did you have trouble finding it? I know it can be…

HELEN. I did the rental car thing and then I'm like, "Okay so should I use the valet?" because I can never remember if that's a good idea or if I should find street parking. What I should have done is park it at the hotel and take a taxi but I like having my own car when I travel. I just like feeling like I have some agency.

MARCUS. A lot of people use Uber these days.

HELEN. Funny how whenever a company becomes the best thing ever, all my friends send me articles about how evil they are. Confirms my suspicions about something, business models or something. But still, I have the car, and I'm like a goldfish. I always think that I should use the car and then I have this exact same conversation with whomever I'm meeting. Really, I could write down everything I say to most people, and just hand it to them, and skip the first ten minutes.

MARCUS. I get it. I understand. You didn't keep me waiting long. I just got here.

HELEN. You're sweet.

MARCUS. I don't know if I'm sweet.

HELEN. Well, maybe I don't know you very well.

MARCUS. Maybe you don't.

HELEN. Definitely I don't.

MARCUS. Definitely you don't.

HELEN. We'll fix that. We'll fix that won't we?

MARCUS. Maybe so. I hope so. Thanks for the...

*(**HELEN** looks at her phone.)*

HELEN. Noisemakers. It's...

(She reads.)

MARCUS. If you want to take a...

HELEN. *(Typing as she speaks.)* I have to... I'm sorry. Do you mind if I just write back to this?

MARCUS. Go ahead.

HELEN. It's rude, I know it's rude.

MARCUS. Go ahead. It's okay.

HELEN. You don't mind?
MARCUS. I don't mind.
HELEN. It won't take long.
MARCUS. Go ahead.
HELEN. Done.
> *(Pause.)*

So.
MARCUS. I asked them to wait until you got here to take our order.
HELEN. Oh. Well, I think they see me now. I'm sure they'll…
> *(Looking over her shoulder.)*

MARCUS. I brought you his sister's number.
HELEN. Oh.
MARCUS. And her e-mail. If that's easier.
HELEN. Thank you.
> *(Silence.)*

MARCUS. You know, we can wait to…
HELEN. No, no. It's all right.
> *(Pause.)*

Noisemakers!
> *(She takes her phone out again.)*

MARCUS. She would be happy to…
HELEN. *(Half-reading.)* Uh-huh.
MARCUS. She wouldn't mind hearing from you.
HELEN. Did she tell you that?
MARCUS. She didn't say so directly. But I can tell.
HELEN. What did she actually say? Because I'm pretty sure she would mind.
> *(Pause.)*

I would mind. If I were her. I would.
MARCUS. She didn't even hesitate to give me her contact information.

HELEN. I'm sorry, didn't you have it already?

MARCUS. When I asked if I could give it to you.

HELEN. Didn't even hesitate.

MARCUS. She didn't. I think she wouldn't mind.

> *(Pause.)*

Whatever happened before...

HELEN. No, it's not that. It's...

> *(Pause.)*

I'm sorry. One second.

> *(She types on her phone.)*

It's about my flight. My coordinator says that my...

> *(Pause.)*

Well I guess you don't need to know.

MARCUS. It's. Yes. It sounds important.

HELEN. I'll put it away.

MARCUS. If it's important. It's a flight. It sounds like you need to focus on it.

HELEN. You know what? I'm going to get up, go call her, come back, and then we can really talk. I want to just be here now. Okay?

MARCUS. Okay.

HELEN. Then you can tell me all about what Tamara thinks about me.

MARCUS. Maybe it's not my place to...

HELEN. Hold that thought.

> *(She stands up, presses a button, and puts the phone to her ear.)*

MARCUS. Holding. Holding.

> *(She exits.)*

Holding that thought.

> *(Blackout.)*

Scene Two

(A few moments later.)
*(**HELEN** and **MARCUS** are sitting together.)*
(There is a bottle of wine on the table.)

HELEN. Again, again, I'm sorry.

MARCUS. It's all right.

HELEN. You know how these things are. Travel.

MARCUS. I guess I do.

HELEN. You guess?

MARCUS. Well I couldn't say.

> *(Pause.)*

HELEN. Again, thank you.

MARCUS. I don't think there's any reason to thank me.

HELEN. This was all very last-minute.

MARCUS. I expected you to call.

HELEN. Well, here I am. Expectations met.

MARCUS. Absolutely. Met.

HELEN. Yes.

> *(She takes a sip of wine.)*

Are you...

> *(Pause.)*

I'm honestly not sure. I'm...

> *(Pause.)*

Have you had this before?

MARCUS. No.

HELEN. Why did you choose it?

MARCUS. Guesswork. Informed guesswork. Everyone actually likes Merlot.

HELEN. Well, I do like it. But I don't think of myself as someone who likes Merlot.

MARCUS. What sort of wine drinker are you?

HELEN. One who drinks beer.

   (Pause.)

Sorry, I'm being. That wasn't meant to be. It was meant to be a joke.

MARCUS. I thought it was funny but I didn't laugh.

HELEN. I do that sometimes.

MARCUS. I used to pretend to laugh for the benefit of other people.

HELEN. When did you stop?

MARCUS. I don't remember. But I did.

   (A sip of wine helps him end the moment.)

HELEN. Well. Either way. Here we are.

   (Pause.)

Here I am.

   *(**MARCUS** smiles a little.)*

MARCUS. I'm sorry the memorial didn't work with your schedule.

HELEN. God, I know how that sounds. Monstrous. But why apologize to me? How could that possibly be your fault?

MARCUS. Someone should have called you.

HELEN. Yes, but is that your fault?

MARCUS. I should have checked with you. I know I should have. I had trouble finding you.

HELEN. I can't see how. I'm on LinkedIn, I'm on Facebook, I'm practically the cover girl for…I guess…the NSA.

   (Pause.)

These things are what they are. You did what you could do. I haven't been in touch. Five years is…

   (Pause.)

Five years is five years.

MARCUS. Still.

HELEN. Five years is five years. I wasn't the…

(Pause.)

I don't know. Thank you for...

(Pause.)

Thank you. You don't have to apologize. Thank you.

(Pause.)

So do you like Los Angeles?

MARCUS. I've lived here for fifteen years. So I guess I like it. There's evidence that I like it.

HELEN. I don't really like it here.

MARCUS. You do a lot of work here?

HELEN. A lot. What's a lot?

MARCUS. Do you visit L.A. often?

HELEN. Why do you ask?

MARCUS. I don't know the answer to the question, I guess. So I figured, find out. Learn about Helen, I thought to myself.

HELEN. I'm here a couple of times a year.

MARCUS. That seems to be frequently.

HELEN. But I never know when I'll be here. So I never...

(Pause.)

I never call ahead.

MARCUS. Hotels and conference rooms.

HELEN. Exactly.

MARCUS. Which hotel are you in?

HELEN. It might be the Sheraton? I'd have to look.

MARCUS. Whenever you're in town, we have a lot of space. If you want to stay with us.

HELEN. That's a nice offer.

MARCUS. Honestly. We're family.

HELEN. I'm not even family with my family.

(Pause.)

MARCUS. Well, I'm sorry we don't know each other better.

HELEN. We should have. I guess.

MARCUS. We're working on it.
HELEN. Let's just...

>*(Pause.)*

Yes.

>*(Pause.)*

Working on it.

>*(Pause.)*

Do you want to share something with the group?

>*(She gestures to the invisible support group.)*

MARCUS. I don't really like the Sheraton. They charge for Wi-Fi.
HELEN. You stay at hotels in your own city?
MARCUS. It is something I have done.
HELEN. There must be a story behind that.
MARCUS. Yes.
HELEN. What is the story behind that?
MARCUS. I am not divorced, but I was almost divorced.
HELEN. Why didn't you get divorced?
MARCUS. Because my wife loves me.
HELEN. That's an interesting way to put it.
MARCUS. Is it?
HELEN. Yes.

>*(Pause.)*

I thought you'd say because you love your wife.
MARCUS. Isn't it the same thing?
HELEN. I guess so. I'm not trying to trip you up.
MARCUS. Anyway, that's why I have hotel preferences.
HELEN. Yes. Well, you're not alone. I'm always in the air or in some lobby. Sometimes, I see people at the same Holiday Inns over and over and they've started to get comfortable or know the staff or have a favorite room. People who say things like, "I believe I'm already in the system as a Premiere Club Member." Those people have

found themselves at home halfway between home and work. I don't know what to make of that. I think that a human being's energy is infused, or infused is the wrong word, but...

(Pause.)

I guess what I'm trying to say is that I spend too much time in hotels. But it's an alternative to living in a box in the city anyway. At least now I can have a house anywhere, like New Hampshire, and it doesn't matter.

MARCUS. Hey you know, I saw you on that show. What was that show?

HELEN. You saw that?

MARCUS. Everyone saw that. You slayed.

HELEN. Well, they didn't understand the science.

MARCUS. Neither do I. But I know there *is* science.

HELEN. Well, there you go. You've got one-up on half the country. More than half.

*(**HELEN** looks at her phone a little too long.)*

I'm going to put this away.

MARCUS. If there's something. I'm resisting the urge, so I get it. I'm getting the night off.

HELEN. I'm a little vacation. How nice for you. But it's not something. It's a habit. There's nothing. Or, more accurately, there's always something. Which transforms it all into a big nothing.

(She puts the phone into her bag.)

MARCUS. We've never really done this, you know?

HELEN. You were always really Jim's friend.

(Pause.)

He always...

MARCUS. He compartmentalized.

HELEN. Yes.

MARCUS. I know that wasn't...

HELEN. I don't think I'm quite there yet. I'm sorry. I can't talk about this yet. Is that all right?

(Pause.)

MARCUS. Yes.

(Pause.)

I don't really travel that much. I wanted to, and thought I would. But Edie just isn't all that good on a plane. Even now. She's never been an easy kid. I love her.

HELEN. Which you have to say.

MARCUS. Which I feel. And want to say.

HELEN. I just meant whenever someone is about to say something critical about their kids, they say, "Oh I really love them," and then proceed to make having children sound really, really exhausting.

MARCUS. Sure, well... Edie is hard on airplanes. The last time I was at a hotel, it was probably a Best Western and I probably just watched *Law & Order* and slept.

HELEN. It's what there is to do. In those rooms.

MARCUS. One of the things.

HELEN. The main thing.

MARCUS. But as I say, we don't fly.

HELEN. It loses its charm.

MARCUS. Well, at least you're out there fighting the good fight.

HELEN. Fighting anyway. Fighting. For a living. Like a volunteer Marine. Ooh-Rah.

(Pause.)

Jim used to talk about Edie all the time. You know.

MARCUS. He would make up stories for her.

(Pause.)

I'd forgotten about that.

HELEN. Well. Fiction was his forte.

(Blackout.)

Scene Three

(Later.)

(Picked-over appetizers are on the table.)

HELEN. *(Referring to the food:)* This is good.

MARCUS. "Small Plates" is my religion. My sister used to own this place, actually.

HELEN. Really?

MARCUS. Indeed.

HELEN. She doesn't anymore?

MARCUS. We still know the owners. She moved to Montana.

HELEN. *(Raised eyebrow.)* Montana.

MARCUS. It is a real place. There are people in it. They have a governor.

HELEN. Name the governor.

MARCUS. What am I, his father?

(Pause.)

HELEN. Ever visited your sister in "Montana"?

MARCUS. No. We don't visit. We're not close that way.

HELEN. My brother calls almost every day.

MARCUS. That's nice.

HELEN. Not really. He's got some serious problems. But he's got no one else, so I sometimes actually pick up the phone.

MARCUS. Only sibling?

HELEN. Yes. Although if I had more, he wouldn't leave much room for them.

MARCUS. I have one older sister and four brothers.

HELEN. Do all of your brothers own restaurants?

MARCUS. No, but they do live in Montana.

HELEN. A picture is forming.

MARCUS. Yes, they do all own cowboy hats.

HELEN. You poor man.

MARCUS. I own a cowboy hat too.

HELEN. A disguise.

MARCUS. A disguise.

HELEN. So everyone is there but you.

MARCUS. 'Tis true. Although none of us is from there.

HELEN. Where are you all from?

MARCUS. California.

HELEN. You must have done something pretty awful to be the last man standing in California.

MARCUS. Restraining orders. Lots of them. To protect me.

(Pause.)

My sister and I get along really well when we don't talk to each other.

HELEN. And yet, here we are. At the restaurant she once owned.

MARCUS. I'm sentimental.

(Pause.)

So how much do you know?

HELEN. I'm not sure what you mean.

MARCUS. About how Jim died.

(Pause.)

HELEN. Oh that. That old thing. That old thing. How much do I know? I guess I know the most important thing. But God is in the details.

MARCUS. I think they say the devil is in the details.

HELEN. Don't fucking correct me. I'm navigating.

MARCUS. I'm really trying not to upset you.

HELEN. I'm going to be upset. There's really nothing to be done about it.

(Pause.)

So what exactly are you asking me?

MARCUS. I think I'm asking if there's anything you don't know, that you want to know.

HELEN. To answer that question, I would need a diagram.

MARCUS. Did you talk to him, before?

HELEN. We certainly didn't talk after.

MARCUS. I... How would you like me to ask this question?

HELEN. I can't help you there. I don't want to be asked this question at all. Maybe we should drop the entire concept of want. Want doesn't factor into any of this at all. I'm doing what I am obligated to do, not what I want to do.

(Pause.)

Is this how you wanted to spend your night off, away from Edie? Having a seance over small plates?

(Pause.)

MARCUS. Why don't I just tell you the story and if you hear things you already know, we'll just chalk that up to living.

HELEN. Is there a lot to know? Is it a long story?

MARCUS. Well... I imagine that depends on when you want me to start the story.

HELEN. Does it start with me?

MARCUS. I think it probably starts even before that.

HELEN. I don't need to know that part. I wasn't there. Then again, when I was with Jim, I don't remember you being there. So, maybe neither of us is a great judge on which parts of the story are key details.

(Pause.)

I'm going to commit to some of my worst impulses and order more wine whenever that waiter comes back from his smoke break. Or wherever he is.

MARCUS. That's up to you.

HELEN. You'll have more? If I get more?

*(**MARCUS** is already late getting home.)*

MARCUS. ...Absolutely.

HELEN. You're late.

MARCUS. Let's have more wine.

HELEN. You don't want more wine.
MARCUS. Let's have more.
HELEN. Do you really want more?
MARCUS. Maybe we should drop the entire concept of want.
HELEN. Should I say touché?
MARCUS. I think you should have more wine.
HELEN. You'll have to join me.
MARCUS. I'll join you.
HELEN. Good. Please. Join me.

(Blackout.)

Scene Four

(**HELEN** *is alone at the table, drinking wine.* **MARCUS** *is up from the table, probably at the restroom.*)

(*She reaches down to her bag and then waves at it like, "Forget it, no."*)

(*Another sip of wine, alone.*)

(*She makes a face at the other empty seat. Incredulous maybe. Wide-eyed. She makes herself laugh.*)

(*Blackout.*)

Scene Five

*(**MARCUS** and **HELEN** at the table. Entrées are now on the table. **HELEN** eats while **MARCUS** tells the story.)*

MARCUS. There's this threshold when you stop complimenting weight loss. It usually comes with other factors, like something is wrong with his teeth. Hair's thinner. Other things. Jim was fine, and then he lost weight, and then he looked like he was hollowing out. He was gray in places that he used to be green.

(Pause.)

Let me take it back a little bit. Um.

(Pause.)

He moved out here and we were all happy about it because, you know, he's near us and that's great. He was not doing well, sent those long e-mails that he'd send. Those e-mails people send when their meds aren't properly calibrated. He'd curse a lot. That's what I always said. He was the kind of guy that cursed to make a joke, usually. When he was off, though, everyone was a motherfucker, or a fucking bitch, or something like that. It was *off*, you know. So we were happy he came out here. Sunshine. We could feed him. That's what we thought.

(Pause.)

Anyway, he would lie. He told me he had hepatitis. He did not have hepatitis. We'd invite him over and he would just not show up. He could drive but said he didn't want to have a car. He sold his car. This is L.A. He'd walk everywhere. Until he sort of stopped going places very far from his home.

(Pause.)

I used to actually have this e-mail chain with my wife and this other friend of his about what to do, you know? We couldn't force him to go to the hospital. He never did anything in front of us that was actually criminal. He wasn't even being dangerous. He was warm. Grateful. But then, he'd disappear. So we were like: "Do we go over there and go through his stuff?" What do we do? I know he went to a lot of groups, but, you know, where were they? We even thought about having him followed.

HELEN. But you didn't do that.

MARCUS. I mean, no. We just talked about it. Who thinks that's actually going to be necessary, you know?

(Pause.)

So…I…

(Pause.)

Well to make it a shorter story, I found out he'd been in and out of the hospital. I literally thought, "At least he's going to the hospital." I took it as a good sign. Then, he died. He went in, and didn't come out.

(Pause.)

So…there's more to it. I don't know what you want to know. But, yes. That's what happened. Right before New Year's Eve.

HELEN. Thank you.

(Pause.)

I'm sorry, I'm the only one eating. I feel bad. You should eat.

MARCUS. I've been talking. So it's all right.

HELEN. Do you mind? I want to try the duck.

(She reaches across the table and takes a bit of food from his plate with her fork.)

MARCUS. No. I don't mind.

(She takes a bite.)

HELEN. Thank you.

(Pause.)

This is a great restaurant.

(Blackout.)

Scene Six

(Later in the meal.)

HELEN. We met at work.

MARCUS. That's what I thought. But I couldn't remember how.

HELEN. Didn't he tell you?

MARCUS. I thought it was because of that PR job. Didn't you both fly to Edmonton and get stuck there?

HELEN. Edmonton? As in Canada?

MARCUS. That wasn't you?

HELEN. Was it someone? Who did he meet in Canada?

MARCUS. Did I just step in it?

HELEN. You might have. You might have. Who did he meet in Canada?

MARCUS. Maybe no one.

HELEN. Well it wasn't me. How do you not even know? We were married for three years.

MARCUS. He told me things. He did. He told me plenty.

HELEN. Do you know my maiden name? Where I grew up?

MARCUS. Did you forget your password or something?

HELEN. What did he tell you exactly?

MARCUS. Things about you. What you did for a living. Do for a living. He told me that you...

HELEN. No, wait. Let's try this another way. We both know he didn't tell you anything. Or just a few small things. So, based on what you did know, what do you think? Tell me my life story and I'll tell you yours. According to James.

*(**MARCUS** takes a deep breath. This seems like a minefield.)*

MARCUS. Doesn't that seem...?

HELEN. We'll name it like a board game. We'll call it Misconception! If I had some dice, I'd totally roll them.

MARCUS. This seems like making fun of him.

HELEN. It's not like we can hurt his feelings.

MARCUS. I don't know.

HELEN. Just give it a go. You look like a goer. You played beer pong or something. This is nothing.

(Pause.)

MARCUS. I...okay. Fine. So...your name is Helen Lachmann, but I used to think it was Lynch, like Jane Lynch. You met Jim at work...

HELEN. No, that comes after. I told you that. You thought we met in Edmonton doing PR. So let's stick with that. And how about the fictional Helen Lynch. Let's hang our hats on that, okay? You meet Helen Lachmann afterwards.

MARCUS. This is absolutely a...

HELEN. Should I start?

MARCUS. You go first. You go first if you actually want to do this.

HELEN. You're Marcus and you've known Jim since you met at the University of Delaware in 199...5? 1994? Your daughter is Edie, and your wife is something like Kikki. Something that sounds Australian to me. Maybe she even is Australian. I have no idea how you met her or what she does. Jim told me a story that the two of you used to walk around your campus with Big Gulps of something purple and eventually puke it up in various young women's rooms in college. You moved to Los Angeles in order to... I have no idea. I don't know why you moved here. But now you work in...distribution? Is that a thing to work in?

(Pause.)

And that's it.

MARCUS. Well you know more than that.

HELEN. That's most of it.

MARCUS. My wife's name is Lenni. And she's not Australian. I develop social media strategies for sort of middle-market stuff. Shows where the audience isn't as plugged in – urban and rural audiences. And I don't like this.

HELEN. What don't you like?

MARCUS. The point you're trying to make.

HELEN. You're sharp. I can see why they let you speak to farmers and people who are "urban."

(Pause.)

I'm...

MARCUS. It's okay. It's okay.

HELEN. Did you think I was about to apologize.

MARCUS. Yes.

HELEN. I guess I was. I guess I was. But maybe just let me get there first.

(Pause.)

So. It's your turn.

MARCUS. I don't want a turn.

HELEN. Should I keep going?

MARCUS. I'd rather you didn't.

HELEN. I know how you feel. I'm tired of the sound of my own voice too.

MARCUS That's not how I feel.

HELEN. How do you feel?

MARCUS. Tired.

HELEN. Yes. Yes, yes. Tired.

(She overturns the bottle and taps out the last of the wine into her glass.)

Oh no. Look at that. I'm probably drunk but I cannot tell.

(She sips.)

Funny story. Apparently, there are types of poisonous spiders that give men an erection right before you die. I met a writer that told me that story, right before we were both interviewed about conservation in the Congo. Do you think he was coming on to me, because, you know, I couldn't tell.

(Pause.)

I don't really date, you know. I don't. I don't really date. It's hard to date. I'm never really at home.

(Pause.)

Did he have a girlfriend?

MARCUS. For a while.

HELEN. Did he meet her in Edmonton?

MARCUS. I don't know where they met, actually.

HELEN. Did you like her?

MARCUS. I do like her. She and Lenni are friends. Became friends. They go out and do things.

HELEN. What was her name?

MARCUS. Is.

HELEN. What is her name?

MARCUS. Tracy.

HELEN. Jim and Tracy. Was she with him when he got sick?

MARCUS. I think there was some overlap, but they'd been broken up for a while.

HELEN. Okay.

(Pause.)

That's okay, I think.

MARCUS. I mean, it was a long time.

HELEN. I don't really date. And there have been times I blame him for that.

(She raises a glass.)

Here's to Tracy, who is not from Canada. May she move on forever, and never look back. May everyone know her name by heart.

(Blackout.)

Scene Seven

*(**MARCUS** at the table alone. He's on the phone.)*

MARCUS. *(On the phone:)* Put Mommy on the...put Mommy on the phone. Can you put Mommy on the phone? That's good! Wow. How many are there? I love... That's good. Can I talk to...

(To Mommy:)

Hi.

(Pause.)

I know, I know, I know. She's processing, and I'm... processing and I'll be done when I'm...

(Pause.)

In the ladies'. I think. On the phone.

(Pause.)

No I didn't tell her that and I'm not going to.

(Pause.)

Well what time in the... Well how can we both...

*(**HELEN** returns to the table and makes a "Go ahead don't mind me" gesture. She sips her wine.)*

I have to run sweetie. It's... No I really have to go –

(Pause.)

She's right here.

*(To **HELEN**:)*

Lenni says hi and sorry for your loss.

HELEN. Thank you.

MARCUS. *(To the phone:)* She says thank you. Okay, I should go. We'll work it out. We'll work it out.

(Pause.)

We'll work it out. I know I know. We'll work it out.

(Pause.)

Well I can't do that but we can work it out. We can work it out.

(Pause.)

Can I just...

(Pause.)

We can work it out.

(Pause.)

We can... We can work it out. Yes, we can work it out.

(Now to Edie:)

Okay... Okay goodnight baby. Can you just tell...

*(**MARCUS** listens for a second and then puts the phone away.)*

Hung up.

HELEN. Everything okay?

MARCUS. Of course. Being a parent is a series of interrupted thoughts.

HELEN. Like being on Fox News.

MARCUS. Right, exactly.

(Pause.)

So we...

HELEN. I wish I had known about the memorial but you know... I couldn't have been here for it anyway. And I wouldn't have known anyone and that would have been really, really...the saddest thing that ever happened to me in my entire life probably. So welcome to the only memorial that I will be attending for my ex-husband. Cheers.

*(Another drink. **MARCUS** does not take a sip.)*

You know, even at the very end of everything for us, after we hashed it all out and did a little nostalgic tour of what we once had and closed the book on it all, you know what he did?

MARCUS. I don't.

HELEN. He said, "I think someday, we'll be together again." Right to my fucking face. As I got my goddamned shoes on so I could never talk to him again. I thought about that all the time. How could I not? I thought about it all the time. And it was just a thing to *say*. Just a thing to say in the moment. Because if he'd meant it, do you think we'd even be sitting here?

MARCUS. I didn't know that.

HELEN. That's why I'm telling you.

MARCUS. The thing is…sometimes the same things that made him so difficult were the things that made people love him. He would just drop in out of nowhere, you know? He was…

HELEN. He wasn't anyone special.

MARCUS. Sure he was.

HELEN. He was barely even special to *me*.

> *(Pause.)*

Jesus, that sounds so dramatic. Oh Lord. I'm sorry. That sounded really dramatic.

> *(Laughing:)*

This is why we didn't… This is exactly the problem. The man was a Rorschach test.

MARCUS. It's okay. It really is.

HELEN. It should make me sad.

MARCUS. Doesn't it make you sad?

HELEN. Not really. Not as much as it should. But it is. It is sad.

> *(**MARCUS** watches **HELEN** for a moment. She's looking away, thinking.)*

MARCUS. Oh, let me give you Tamara's e-mail address.

HELEN. How are you doing?

MARCUS. Me?

HELEN. Are you okay?

MARCUS. I'm not great.

HELEN. I mean in general. About all this.

MARCUS. I'm really angry with him. But I'm not allowed to be, because I'm playing priest to everyone who's surprised he died.

   (Pause.)

If a friend gets lung cancer, it might be a death sentence. Still, we circle the wagons. Everything that can be done, is done. The patient gets a schedule, fights it, tries to live. Takes pills. Makes decisions. Talks to everyone about those decisions. That's lung cancer. Addiction isn't like that. It convinces you not to save your own life.

   (Pause.)

Anyway, I know you're angry with him, and I respect that. But you weren't here. You can't imagine how many of us spent hours trying to get a bucket under the parts of him that were falling off.

   (Pause.)

I couldn't have him around Edie because she was scared of him. He looked like a monster in a movie. He'd show up to restaurants and he looked so bad that I'd have to convince the waiters that yes, I was meeting this man, and no, he wasn't bothering me.

   (Pause.)

Then I'm making all these phone calls so people he knew don't find out on Facebook. This liar and addict and sociopath has me going out to dinner with his ex-wife. I think, you know, didn't he care about what this was like for anyone else?

   (Pause.)

I guess that's the answer. Some version of the answer. The answer right now.

HELEN. I understand.

MARCUS. I don't know. Maybe you do. Maybe.

HELEN. Maybe I don't.
MARCUS. Thank you for saying it anyway.
HELEN. It was easy.
>*(Pause.)*

But you're welcome.
>*(Pause.)*

Did you say any of that at the man's funeral?
MARCUS. Fuck no I did not. I didn't say anything.
HELEN. Were there a lot of people there?
MARCUS. Yes.
HELEN. But not me.
MARCUS. Yes.
HELEN. Was it conspicuous?
MARCUS. I don't think most people noticed.
HELEN. How many of these dinners have you hosted?
MARCUS. Like this? One.
>*(Pause.)*

Just you.
>*(Pause.)*

It's nice to finally meet you.
>*(Blackout.)*

Scene Eight

(Very late. **MARCUS** *and* **HELEN** *are now laughing and smiling.)*

HELEN. *(Laughing.)* She did!

MARCUS. I can't believe that.

HELEN. That's the thing! It's not just on television she acts like that. Plus, all she drinks is Diet Coke. Like it's surgically attached to her arm.

MARCUS. She is very skinny.

HELEN. It's a Reagan-era diet. One of the many Reagan-era things about her, besides her politics.

MARCUS. She's not putting it on?

HELEN. She is not. She really did say it. I mean, there weren't cameras, we were in the green room.

MARCUS. That's frightening.

HELEN. I don't know. I liked it. I've always hated her. I liked having my suspicions confirmed.

MARCUS. People *agree* with her. That's what scares me.

(A sip of coffee.)

Okay, okay so I have to know. Why does Tamara…

HELEN. Why does she hate me?

MARCUS. Yes. Why does she hate you.

HELEN. Trade secret.

MARCUS. No, no, no. Come on. She clearly…

HELEN. We've been talking tonight. Do you like me?

MARCUS. That's a trick question.

HELEN. How is that a trick question?

MARCUS. This is not a normal evening.

HELEN. Do you like me?

MARCUS. Sure I do.

HELEN. It was a trick question.

MARCUS. I knew it.

HELEN. But now I forget the rest of the trick. Isn't that always the way? Where is she these days?

MARCUS. You're changing the subject.

HELEN. I'm not. We're still talking about her.

MARCUS. She lives here.

HELEN. She lives in L.A.?

MARCUS. Well, about an hour outside.

HELEN. I thought you were going to say New York City.

MARCUS. No, she's here.

HELEN. How did she handle all this?

MARCUS. I don't know. She just seemed pissed off. She's hard to read. Then again, she's busy, and not very engaged. She's got a family, two kids.

HELEN. Someone married her?

MARCUS. Someone, yes. But I get the impression that she's got her thing – her life – and she sort of just lives it.

HELEN. Sounds familiar.

MARCUS. Weren't they both army brats? Or all of them?

HELEN. He's the youngest. Was the youngest.

(Pause.)

Anyway, their parents both died when they were really young. I think. I actually don't know how they died. He never talked about it.

MARCUS. That can't have been good for anyone.

HELEN. Probably not. But they all did okay for themselves.

MARCUS. I actually think, at this point, that's a hard statement to make.

(Pause.)

You changed the subject.

HELEN. No, it changed itself.

MARCUS. Isn't there a story?

HELEN. Why does there have to be?

MARCUS. You would just say, "There's no story," if there was no story.

HELEN. There's no story.

MARCUS. Now I don't believe you.

HELEN. Under the advisement of my counsel, I shall make no further statements at this time.

MARCUS. So what did you do to Tamara?

HELEN. I didn't do anything. It wasn't my fault.

MARCUS. What wasn't? What didn't you do?

HELEN. I didn't love Jim very much.

>   *(Pause.)*

Maybe at all, really.

MARCUS. That's not very funny.

HELEN. Not it's not very funny. No. It isn't. I thought it was going to be, but then I said it.

>   *(Pause.)*

I think she… I think she thinks he reached out to me and that I could have helped him.

MARCUS. He called you?

HELEN. All the time.

MARCUS. When?

HELEN. All the time.

MARCUS. I didn't know that.

HELEN. Well. Well well. Well. Yes. He did. I hadn't talked to him in years. For a reason. He wasn't my lost love. He would call me, and I would think, "Why does he keep calling me?" I didn't want to see him. I don't want to talk about him like he was someone I'll miss. I guess I didn't ever love him at all, honestly. He was a habit I formed, but then I broke that habit.

>   *(Pause.)*

I mean, if I loved him I would have answered the phone or responded to e-mails.

But I did not, and I never would have, and even now, I'm glad I didn't. I didn't want to be involved. I still don't. I'm here because you asked me to be, because

I was curious, maybe. You seem nice. A better friend than he deserves. Deserved.

(Pause.)

HELEN. Anyway, I get the impression that Tamara thought if I had maybe talked to him or picked up the phone or bothered to whatever-it-is she thinks I could have done, he'd be okay right now. But of course, he wouldn't be. He wasn't even doing well when we were married. Before we were married he lied to me. Even then.

(Pause.)

She thinks I don't care that he died. I'm not even sure that I do.

MARCUS. You know…

(Pause.)

I lost someone I did love. Even if you didn't.

(Pause.)

So, I don't know.

HELEN. You wanted to have dinner. This is dinner.

MARCUS. There are some things…not to say. That you shouldn't tell other people.

(Pause.)

There are things to keep to yourself.

(Blackout.)

Scene Nine

(Check is on the table.)

HELEN. I can put it on a card.

MARCUS. We can just split it.

HELEN. Let me pay for this.

MARCUS. That's not necessary.

HELEN. I should pay for it.

MARCUS. I'd really prefer you didn't.

(Pause.)

I'm the one that invited you, and had you jump through all these, well, hoops. So…why don't I pay for it?

HELEN. We can split it.

MARCUS. I didn't bring cash.

HELEN. They'll cut cards down the middle.

MARCUS. That's fine.

HELEN. But I'm the one who ordered all that wine. You shouldn't pay the same as…

MARCUS. It doesn't matter.

*(**MARCUS** takes the check and puts his card down on it.)*

HELEN. Are you…

MARCUS. It doesn't even matter. Let's not do this dance.

HELEN. You know. No. No. I'm going to pay for this.

(She takes his card off the bill and holds it to him.)

I insist.

MARCUS. Can we just…

HELEN. I insist. I insist.

*(**MARCUS** takes his card back and then rises.)*

MARCUS. All right then. If that's what you want. If… Well if I'm not involved in this last bit, do you mind if I head home? I'm late for the… I should be home.

*(**HELEN** rises as well.)*

HELEN. So.

    (Pause.)

All right so.

    (Pause.)

So thank you.

MARCUS. That's all right.

HELEN. We'll…well. Yes. Apologize to your family for my keeping you out so late.

MARCUS. I'll pass that along.

    (He gathers his coat.)

HELEN. Thank you then.

MARCUS. No need to thank me.

    (He holds out his hand for her to shake.)

Good luck with everything.

    (She takes his hand and shakes it.)

Goodnight then.

HELEN. Right goodnight. Do you mind if I…

    (Pause.)

Do you mind if I give you a hug?

    (Pause.)

You know, never mind.

MARCUS. That would be all right. If you need to do that.

HELEN. I just feel like a *handshake*, you know?

MARCUS. You don't have to explain.

HELEN. God, I'm sorry.

MARCUS. Why don't you just go ahead? I have to go.

    (Pause.)

Go ahead.

    (Pause.)

Or I can…

(She hugs him, a bit awkwardly.)

*(**MARCUS** allows this. Then, in a tiny moment of generosity, he moves to make the hug less awkward.)*

All right then. So.

(They separate.)

(He reaches his hand out again.)

(She takes it and shakes.)

Goodbye.

(She nods.)

*(**MARCUS** exits.)*

(Blackout.)

Scene Ten

(HELEN alone. She's texting at the table. She's got an after-dinner drink.)

(The WAITER appears with the check in his hand.)

(The WAITER is played by the same actor that played JAMES in Act One.)

WAITER. This is just for the drink.

HELEN. Thank you.

WAITER. We're going to start closing.

HELEN. Should I…

WAITER. No, no. You can stay.

   (Pause.)

You know, my ex-boyfriend…

HELEN. I'd just like to…

WAITER. I know but he died, too. He was climbing a tree. If you can believe that.

HELEN. Oh.

   (Pause.)

I can believe that.

WAITER. I overheard. That's all.

HELEN. That's all right.

WAITER. What I'm saying is…you can sit here. If you want. No one's going to rush you out.

HELEN. Thank you.

WAITER. Are you okay?

(HELEN stops and puts down her phone. She actually looks at him for the first time.)

(A moment.)

(A memory.)

HELEN. No.

WAITER. If you want to sit here while we close up…that's fine with me. I'll let them know. It gets really quiet in here once everyone leaves.

HELEN. I don't need to.

WAITER. I'm a waiter.

HELEN. I see that.

WAITER. So I can't promise you that the advice I give will lead you to some high station.

(**HELEN** *smiles.*)

HELEN. Nonetheless…

WAITER. Nonetheless, I…I think you should just sit and have that drink. I promise, I'll come get you, when it's time to go.

(*They look at each other.*)

HELEN. You promise.

WAITER. I promise.

HELEN. I'm going to hold you to that.

(*She smiles just a little.*)

I'll wait here then. For you to come and get me.

(*The* **WAITER** *exits.*)

(**HELEN** *puts her phone away.*)

(*She looks at the empty chair across from her.*)

End of Play

Milton Keynes UK
Ingram Content Group UK Ltd.
UKHW021352010924
1454UKWH00048B/760